This Little Tiger book belongs to:

_____

_____

_____

Especially for Daniel Cautley and Max Henry with love
~ M. C. B.

To Mum and Dad, thank you
And to my little bears, who love their porridge
~ D. H.

LITTLE TIGER PRESS
1 The Coda Centre, 189 Munster Road, London SW6 6AW
www.littletiger.co.uk

First published in Great Britain 2004
by Little Tiger Press, London
This edition published 2013

Text copyright © M. Christina Butler 2004
Illustrations copyright © Daniel Howarth 2004

M. Christina Butler and Daniel Howarth have asserted
their rights to be identified as the author and illustrator of this work
under the Copyright, Designs and Patents Act, 1988

Printed in China • LTP/1900/0687/0613

2 4 6 8 10 9 7 5 3 1

Who's Been Eating My Porridge?

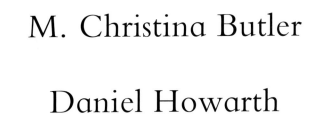

M. Christina Butler

Daniel Howarth

LITTLE TIGER PRESS

Little Bear never ate his porridge.

"All little bears eat porridge," said Mommy Bear. "It makes them big and strong."

But Little Bear shook his head. "No porridge," he said. "No porridge."

"Then I'll give it to Old Scary Bear, who lives in the woods," said Mommy Bear.

And Little Bear watched as Mommy Bear took the porridge outside and left it on an old tree stump.

That day while Mommy and Daddy Bear
gathered honey from the bees, Little Bear
climbed trees and watched out for
Old Scary Bear.

On the way home, Daddy Bear said,
"Did you see Old Scary Bear?"
    "No," replied Little Bear with his nose
in the air, "because there is no Old Scary Bear!"
    "Well, somebody has eaten your porridge,"
said Mommy Bear when they got back
to the bear den.

The next morning Daddy Bear put some honey on Little Bear's porridge, but Little Bear still wouldn't eat it. "I don't like porridge. It's horrible!" he cried.

So Daddy Bear
took it outside
and left it on the
tree stump for
Old Scary Bear.

That day, Grandma and Grandpa Bear came to stay and they all went out to pick berries.

"I hear you don't eat your porridge, Little Bear," said Grandpa Bear as they walked home. "It's no wonder Old Scary Bear has been around. Old Scary Bear loves porridge."

When they arrived back at the
bear den, Little Bear ran over to
the tree stump and found that his
porridge bowl was empty again!

The next morning, Grandma Bear
put some honey and berries on
Little Bear's porridge, but Little
Bear held his nose and closed
his eyes. "No porridge!"
he cried. "I hate porridge!"

And so Grandpa Bear took the porridge
outside for Old Scary Bear.

That day, Little Bear's aunt and uncle and his two cousins came for a visit.

While the grown-up bears gathered nuts in the woods, Little Bear and his cousins played Old Scary Bear games among the trees.

On the way home, Little Bear was very quiet and wouldn't speak to anyone.
"I bet he's tired," said Daddy Bear.

At dinner time, Little Bear wasn't feeling
hungry. Daddy Bear took him upstairs
and tucked him into bed.

That night Little Bear had a bad dream.
Old Scary Bear was chasing him through
the woods.

"I want your porridge," he growled.
"It makes me big and strong!"

Little Bear ran and ran with his porridge . . .
over the fields where the berries grow . . .
through the woods where the nuts grow . . .
and past the hives where the
bees make honey . . .

until he came
to the old tree stump.
"You're not having
my porridge!" he shouted
to Old Scary Bear, and he
sat down and ate up all
his porridge—every bit.

And then he woke up.

The next morning at breakfast,
Little Bear ate a bowl of porridge
with honey . . .

and then he had
a second helping
with nuts and
berries.

All day long Little Bear was very busy. He helped
Grandma Bear and Mommy Bear make berries
into jam and put honey into jars.

Then he went to help Grandpa Bear and Daddy Bear. As they were storing the nuts, Daddy Bear said suddenly, "What's that noise?"

All the bears listened carefully and then they looked outside.

There in front of the bear den were lots of little animals all shouting, "Where's our porridge? Where's our porridge?"

"So *that's* who Old Scary Bear is!" cried Little Bear with a giggle.

And from that day to this one, every morning when Little Bear finishes eating his porridge, he takes another bowl of porridge outside for *Old Scary Bear*. And it always gets eaten!